The Littlest Dinosaur

Terrance Dicks

Illustrated by

Bethan Matthews

PUFFIN BOOKS

PUFFIN BOOKS

Published by the Penguin Group
Penguin Books Ltd, 27 Wrights Lane, London W8 5TZ, England
Penguin Books USA Inc., 375 Hudson Street, New York, New York 10014, USA
Penguin Books Australia Ltd, Ringwood, Victoria, Australia
Penguin Books Canada Ltd, 10 Alcorn Avenue, Toronto, Ontario, Canada M4V 3B2
Penguin Books (NZ) Ltd, 182–190 Wairau Road, Auckland 10, New Zealand

Penguin Books Ltd, Registered Offices: Harmondsworth, Middlesex, England

The Littlest Dinosaur
First published by Hamish Hamilton Ltd 1993

The Littlest On Guard
First published by Hamish Hamilton Ltd 1994

This omnibus edition published in Puffin Books, 1995

1 3 5 7 9 10 8 6 4 2

Filmeset in 15pt Baskerville by Rowland Phototypesetting Ltd

Made and printed in Great Britain by Clays Ltd, St Ives plc

Contents

Chapter One

"'Tis!" shouted Elly.

"'Tisn't!" yelled Olly.

"Quiet, you two!" called their mother.

They were in Mr Orlovsky's antique shop; a long, thin, amazingly untidy room full of – well, it was full of old junk really, but Mr Orlovsky liked to call it antiques. Mrs Elkins, Olly and Elly's mother, was looking at a coffee table.

"Genuine Georgian," said Mr

Orlovsky. "A bargain at ten pounds!"

Mrs Elkins sniffed. "Genuine junk, more like it. Might be worth five . . . "

They were just settling down for a good haggle when they were interrupted by the fuss from the back of the shop. The twins, Oliver and Eleanor, Olly and Elly for short, were arguing again. They'd started fighting as babies in their big twin pram, and had kept it up ever since.

Mrs Elkins sighed. "What are you two fighting about now?" she asked.

"It's this egg," said Elly.

"It's not an egg," said Olly. "Not a real one anyway."

" 'Tis!"

closed

"'Tisn't!"

"Don't start that again!" said their mother. "Bring the thing here and let's have a look at it."

Olly and Elly came forward from the gloom at the back of the shop. Elly was clutching something that certainly looked like an enormous egg. It was very big and a sort of dingy yellow in colour. "We found it in an old chest," explained Elly. "I think it's an ostrich egg.'

"Rubbish," said Olly. "It's made of plaster."

"'Tisn't!"

"'Tis!"

"Hush!" said Mrs Elkins. She turned to Mr Orlovsky. "Well?"

Mr Orlovsky was small and tubby,

with a shining bald head that looked very much like an egg itself. "To be honest, I'm not sure . . . But that chest came from the house of a famous explorer. He travelled all over the world: Africa, China, the North Pole . . ."

Mrs Elkins took the strange object from Elly's hands. It had a rough, leathery feel. "Well, it's certainly not marble or anything like that."

"Can we have it, Mum?" asked Elly eagerly.

Mr Orlovsky seized his chance. "I tell you what. For a favourite customer, with such charming children . . . You give me eight pounds for the table and I throw in the egg for free!"

"Seven!" said Mrs Elkins.

"Seven-fifty?"

"Done!"

"Well," said Olly. "What are you going to do with it?"

They were sitting in the garden, the egg on the grass between them.

"Hatch it!" said Elly firmly.

"What are you going to do – sit on it?" Olly jumped up and down making chicken noises. "You'll look a real twit, perched on a plaster egg!"

"Don't be so silly, Olly. We'll

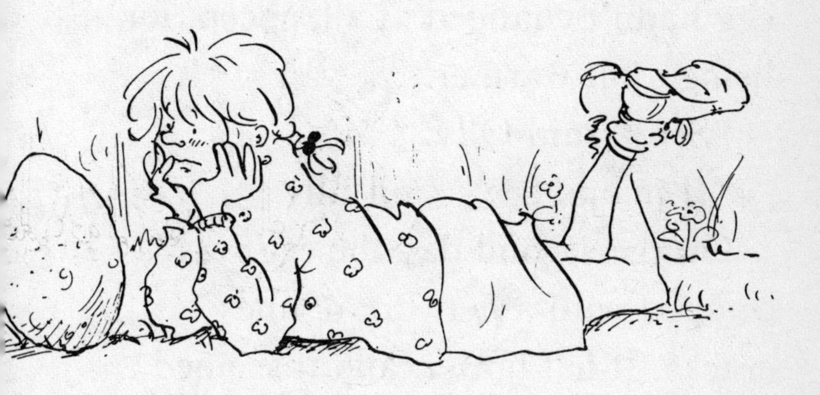

hatch it in Dad's greenhouse!"

Picking up the egg, Elly led the way down the garden and into the greenhouse. The air felt hot and damp and steamy, just like a jungle. They found a big empty plant-pot and put the egg inside, covering it with peat. Then Elly put the pot under a bench, hiding it with a sack.

"We'll come in and check on it every day, when no one's about."

The first time they checked, the egg hadn't changed at all, except for being a bit warmer.

"See?" said Olly.

"*Wait* and see!" said Elly.

On the second day the egg was covered with a network of fine cracks. It felt hotter, and it seemed to be throbbing . . .

"Well?" said Elly triumphantly.

For once, Olly was speechless.

On the third day there were even more cracks. The egg was shaking, and it seemed to be bulging from the inside.

Suddenly the shell cracked open, and a blunt little head popped out. It looked at Elly, and then at Olly.

"Eek!" it said. "Eek!"

Struggling wildly, the little creature kicked itself free of the shell. It had powerful back legs, a long tail, and tiny arms and hands dangling in front of it.

"That's no ostrich," said Olly, puzzled.

"I know," said Elly. "It's a baby dinosaur!"

Chapter Two

The tiny dinosaur looked up at them with bright little eyes. It peered into their faces, looking first at Elly, then at Olly.

"It's imprinting!" whispered Elly. "I saw it on one of those nature programmes. When chicks come out of the shell, they think the first thing they see is their mum. Maybe it works for dinosaurs too!"

"So it thinks we're its mum and dad?"

"That's right."

"Eek!" said the little dinosaur. "Eek! Eek! Eek!"

Its wide open mouth reminded Elly of something else she'd seen on a nature programme – little birds in a nest waiting to be fed.

"I think it's hungry. What do dinosaurs eat?"

Olly scratched his head. "Other dinosaurs?"

"Not to start with, surely . . . " Elly looked round the greenhouse. She went over to a tomato plant and picked a ripe and juicy tomato. "Lend me your penknife, Olly."

She cut the tomato up into little pieces and dropped one into the baby dinosaur's mouth. It gulped it down, looked pleased and said "Eek!" once more. Elly dropped another bit of tomato into the gaping mouth. Then another and another . . .

When the whole tomato was gone, the dinosaur burped happily. Then it rolled over on its back and went to sleep.

Olly looked down at it. "Are you sure it's a dinosaur? It's the littlest dinosaur I've ever seen!"

"That's what we'll call it," said Elly. "We'll call it Littlest!"

"Never mind what we call it, what do we *do* with it? If we leave it here, it'll scoff all Dad's tomatoes."

"Or it might just wake up and run off," said Elly. "We'll have to smuggle it into the house!"

They put the sleeping Littlest in a cardboard box, covered him with a bit of sacking and carried him up to Elly's room.

For the next few days, Littlest lived perfectly happily in the blanket-lined bottom shelf of Elly's toy-cupboard. Olly and Elly spent as much time with him as they could. Their mother was always telling them to eat more fruit, and she was pleased to see that they seemed to be taking notice at last. She didn't realise that the fruit was disappearing into Olly and Elly's pockets – and soon afterwards into Littlest's tummy.

Littlest ate and ate – and grew and grew. Before very long, he'd grown from the size of a chick to that of a chicken.

"This can't go on you know," said Olly one day.

They were watching Littlest playing with a ball from the toy cupboard. It was one of those baby balls with a little bell inside. Littlest loved it. He spent ages kicking it up and down the room with his powerful back legs.

"The only footballing dinosaur in

captivity!" said Elly proudly. "What can't go on?"

"Keeping a pet dinosaur hidden in your bedroom. Look how much it's grown."

Elly rolled the ball away so Littlest could chase it. "So?"

"Well, it'll go on growing, won't it? Growing and growing . . . It'll get too big for the toy cupboard, too big for the room. It'll burst out and go stomping around London smashing down houses. You'll catch it then – Mum will be furious!"

"You've been watching too many monster movies on TV," said Elly.

"And how long is it going to be satisfied with just fruit?" went on Olly. "Any day now it'll start craving meat. And you know what the nearest meat is? Us!"

Olly was going over the top as usual, thought Elly. But perhaps there was *something* in what he was saying.

"We do need to know more about dinosaurs," she agreed. "What they eat, how fast they grow, everything . . ."

"We could try the library," said Olly.

Elly shook her head. "I've got a better idea. There's a special Dinosaur Exhibition at the Natural History Museum. We'll go and visit it. Once we know what kind of dinosaur Littlest is, we can decide what to do."

Chapter Three

"Eek!" said a little voice from Elly's school bag.

"Shut up!" hissed Olly.

Olly and Elly were at the Natural History Museum, waiting in line to enter the Dinosaur Exhibition. They hadn't intended to bring Littlest as well, but when they tried to leave him behind the little dinosaur had made the most tremendous fuss, shrieking "Eek! Eek! Eek!" and scrabbling against the door.

Eventually they'd been forced to give in and bring Littlest with them, tucked into Elly's school bag.

"We'll have had it if anyone finds out Littlest is here in the Museum," whispered Olly.

"I don't see why," said Elly. "What's wrong with bringing a dinosaur to a dinosaur exhibition?"

They moved on through the huge hall. There were illuminated display cases and notice boards, models and skeletons, pictures of dinosaurs of every kind – but none that looked quite like Littlest. There was even a model dinosaur's nest with lots of baby dinosaurs popping out of eggs.

The high spot of the exhibition was a life-size tableau. You went up

some stairs and looked down from a walk-way.

Down below, in a rocky prehistoric landscape, a huge dead dinosaur was being eaten by three smaller ones. Their claws and teeth were red, and they made harsh croaking sounds.

Littlest popped his head out of the bag for a look, gave a horrified "Eek!" and popped back inside.

Olly gave Elly a nudge. "See?"

Elly shuddered. Was Littlest really going to turn into a rampaging monster?

They came out of the exhibition and stopped for tea and buns in a little café area in the main hall of the museum.

A muffled "Eek!" came from the bag. Elly bought an orange, popping segments into the school bag to keep Littlest quiet.

"I've got so much dinosaur information in my brain it feels like bursting," she said.

Olly nodded. "Me too! Nothing that helps with our problem though."

"We could try the book shop."

"Oh sure! Maybe they've got a copy of 'How to Look After Your Pet Dinosaur'!"

"A fat lot of help you are!" said Elly. "All you can do is make silly jokes."

"Well, if you hadn't hatched that egg in the first place . . ."

CAFE

In no time at all, Olly and Elly were off on one of their famous rows. They were so busy arguing that they didn't notice what was happening in the school bag at Elly's feet.

The orange was all finished and Littlest was getting very bored with being shut up. He wriggled his head out of the bag. Then his long neck –

and then the rest of him. Claws clattering on the stone floor, Littlest jumped out of the bag and looked around.

Elly saw what was happening – just too late! She made a grab for Littlest's tail, missing it by inches.

Confused by the chatter of the crowd and the wide open space all around, Littlest panicked. With a

shrill "Eek! Eek! Eek!", the little dinosaur ran away.

The hall was filled with mums and dads and kids who'd come to see the dinosaur exhibition. They hadn't bargained on meeting a real one! There were yells of amazement as Littlest dashed across the big echoing hall.

A dignified-looking lady screamed as Littlest shot between her legs.

An astonished toddler howled and dropped his ice cream as the little dinosaur whizzed by.

An angry old gentleman tried to hook the fleeing Littlest with the handle of his walking stick, but Littlest leaped over the stick and disappeared down a side passage.

Grabbing her bag, Elly chased after him, Olly close behind. They tore down the corridor, past displays of snakes and fishes and lizards, and along a white-walled corridor lined with office doors.

Suddenly they found themselves in another crowded exhibition hall. In the middle of the room there was a life-sized model of a whale, surrounded by elephants and rhinoceroses.

Amidst more shouts and screams, Littlest shot underneath the whale, dodged in and out of the elephants and rhinos, circled right round the hall, and streaked out the way he'd come in.

Olly and Elly panted along behind

him, shoving past astonished museum visitors with shouts of "'Scuse me!" and "Sorry!".

Soon they were chasing Littlest back down the white-walled corridor. A group of tourists appeared, blocking the far end.

"Now we've got him!" yelled Olly – but they hadn't.

There was a flight of stone steps on the left, barred by a "No Entry" barrier. Littlest jumped over the barrier and disappeared up the stairs. Ducking under the bar, Olly and Elly followed.

The steps led them to another corridor much like the first. Just ahead they could see Littlest, still sprinting along.

"He's not even tired," gasped Elly.

"I am," said Olly. "And I've got a stitch. We'll never catch him."

Just then a tall, thin man appeared round the corner, ahead of Littlest. He had big glasses and lots of straggly grey hair. He was reading a book as he walked along, and he didn't notice the little dinosaur – not until he tripped over him! Then he crashed to the ground, falling on top of Littlest who gave an angry "Eek!"

Before Littlest could set off again, Elly ran up and grabbed him.

The tall man picked himself up, blinked and said mildly, "Am I mistaken, or is that a live dinosaur you have there?"

"Well . . . " said Elly.

They heard shouting coming from below – and it was getting nearer. "Maybe we'd better talk in my office," said the tall man.

He led them around the corner, along a smaller corridor and into a tiny cluttered room, filled with books and old bones.

"Now then," he said, closing the door.

"It's like this," said Olly.

"We found this egg," said Elly.

Talking in turn, and sometimes both together, they poured out the whole story.

"Astonishing!" said the tall man. He looked hard at Littlest, who'd jumped down from Elly's lap and was pottering around the room. "But

why did you bring the creature here?"

"We needed to know more about dinosaurs," said Elly.

"Like how long we've got before he grows enormous and starts trampling down buildings and eating people," explained Olly.

The tall man chuckled. "I don't think you need worry about that!"

Elly stared at him. "What do you mean?"

"What you have here is an Eichinodon, one of the smaller dinosaurs. It won't grow much bigger than it is now. And as for eating people – the Eichinodon is a vegetarian."

"Are you sure?" said Olly.

"I happen to be a Professor of Natural History," said the tall man. "Dinosaurs are my special subject – I've been studying them all my life." He tickled Littlest under the chin. "Mind you, this is the first chance I've had to study a live one!"

"Then we can keep him!" said Elly happily.

"What about Mum and Dad?"

asked Olly. "We can't keep Littlest a secret much longer."

"Suppose I write to your parents," suggested the Professor.

"I'll tell them that by looking after Littlest you'll be helping the Museum with important scientific research."

"Wonderful!" said Elly. "They're dead keen on anything educational."

"What about our chasing Littlest round the Museum?" asked Olly. "Won't there be a huge fuss?"

"I doubt it," said the Professor. "When they see something impossible, people just don't believe their eyes. Pretty soon everyone will be convinced it was a dog or a cat or a chicken."

Soon it was all arranged, and Olly and Elly and Littlest were on their way home. On the bus, Littlest popped his head out of the bag, looking around curiously. Luckily they were upstairs in the front seat and nobody noticed.

"He's going to be quite a handful," said Olly.

"Who cares?" said Elly. "Littlest is the only living dinosaur – and he's ours!"

"Eek!" said Littlest happily. "Eek! Eek! Eek!"

The Littlest On Guard

Chapter One

"Chocolate!" shouted Elly.

"Vanilla!" yelled Olly.

"Eek!" said Littlest, joining in.

Olly and Elly were twins. They were in the Superette doing some shopping. Littlest was their pet dinosaur who travelled everywhere with them in Elly's schoolbag. They'd hatched him from a very old egg they'd found in an antique shop.

(If you're wondering how Elly got a whole dinosaur in her schoolbag,

Littlest was a special sort of dinosaur called an Eichinodon. He was about the size of a chicken, and wasn't going to grow much bigger.)

As usual, Olly and Elly were arguing – this time about which flavour ice-cream to buy.

"Why not get Neapolitan," said a voice from above their heads. "Then you get chocolate, vanilla and strawberry, too."

Olly and Elly turned and looked up. Towering above them was a tall thin man with straggly hair and big glasses.

"Professor!" said Elly. "What are you doing here?"

"Eek!" said Littlest. He was very fond of the Professor.

The Professor worked at the Natural History Museum. He had made a special study of dinosaurs and he was helping the twins to look after Littlest. He scratched Littlest under the chin. The little dinosaur yawned and curled up inside the bag for a doze.

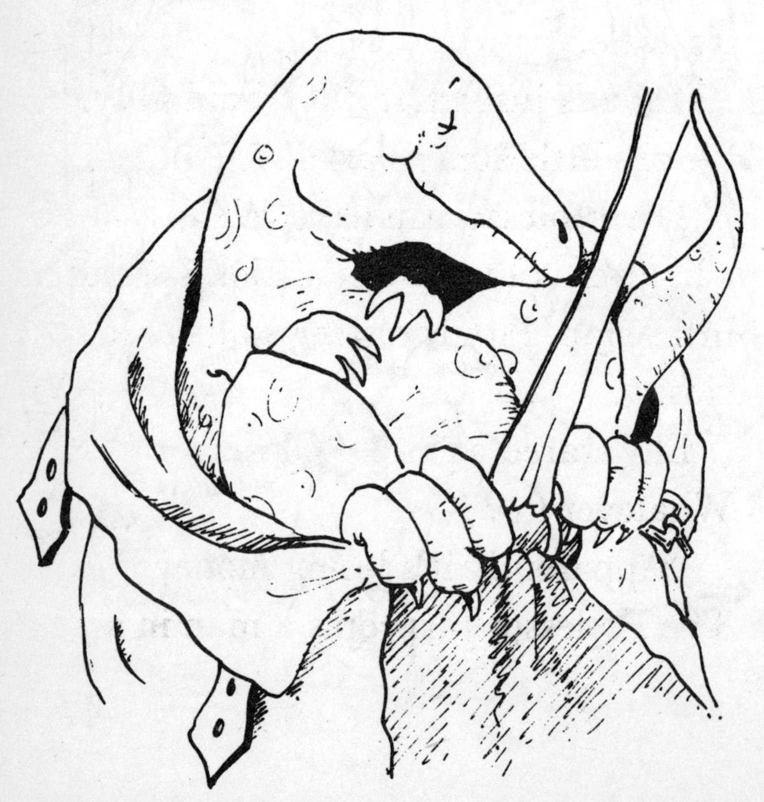

"I'm doing the same as you," said the Professor, answering Elly's question. "Shopping. This is *my* local supermarket as well."

"It's not a supermarket, it's a Superette," said Olly.

"Superette is a nonsense word really," said the Professor. "It means big-little."

"That's just what it is," said Olly. "A big-little supermarket!"

The Professor smiled. "Well, whatever you call it, it's a jolly useful little shop. Pity it's going to have to close."

Elly stared at him. "Close? Whatever for?"

"Apparently it's losing money." The Professor turned as a man in a white coat came down the aisle. "Isn't that right, Mr Patel?"

"I'm afraid it is," answered Mr Patel sadly. "If things go on like this . . . "

"But how can you be losing money?" asked Elly. "The place is always open, and it always seems to be busy."

"Stealing," said Mr Patel. "Every month my profits are down. People must be stealing things instead of buying them."

"Can't you do anything about it?" asked Olly.

"I tried! I even hired a security guard, but it hasn't helped."

Suddenly, a very large young man came marching down the aisle. He

was tubby as well as big, and his blue uniform looked too tight for him. He had a round, cheerful face and floppy fair hair.

"'Scuse me, Mr Patel," he said in a shy, husky voice.

"What is it, Sidney?"

"I've been keeping an eye on these two kids. They've been hanging round here for quite a while. They look a bit suspicious to me."

"Suspicious be blowed," said Olly. "We've just been making up our minds what flavour ice-cream to buy."

"I'm sorry, but I've got my job to do," said the young man obstinately. He turned to Elly. "What have you got in that bag – which happens to be open, I see?"

"None of your business," said Elly.

"Well, there's something in there – something about the size of a nice big chicken. May I have a look, please?"

"I wouldn't if I were you!" said Olly. "You'll be sorry!"

"Oh, will I?" said Sidney. "We'll soon see about that!"

He shoved his hand into the bag, and then pulled it out again.

"Ouch!" he yelled.

Littlest, annoyed at being disturbed, had given him a nasty nip. The little dinosaur popped his head out of the schoolbag and glared at Sidney. "Eek!" he said angrily.

Sidney jumped back. "What is it?"

"It's a man-eating dinosaur," said

Olly. "You'd better watch out! Now he's had a taste of you he might fancy the rest."

Sidney turned and almost ran off down the aisle.

The Professor said, "I take it that was your new security guard?"

Mr Patel nodded. "Sidney's not very experienced, I'm afraid, but he does try." He looked uneasily at Littlest who was glaring after Sidney. "That creature isn't really a man-eater, is it?"

Elly laughed. "Don't worry, Littlest is a vegetarian. He prefers fruit to people."

Mr Patel pulled a banana from a bunch in a rack overhead and handed it to Littlest who took it in his little front paws with an "Eek!" of delight. Mr Patel gave them a smile and moved away. Peeling the banana, Littlest scoffed it up in a few quick bites.

"What a nice man," said Olly. "Shame about all his problems."

"Is that all you can say?" asked Elly.

"What do you mean?" asked Olly. "What are we supposed to do?"

"Help him, of course," said Elly. "We're going to find out who's robbing the Superette!"

Chapter Two

"See that very large lady over there?" said Olly. "The one in the fruit section?"

"What about her?" asked Elly.

"She's not really as big as that – nobody is! I bet she's really a skinny little person wearing a special suit with lots of secret pockets. She buys a few things and pinches a whole lot more . . . "

"Of all the daft ideas," said Elly.

"Eek!" said Littlest, who was

getting bored.

They'd been hanging around in the Superette for ages. Olly and the Professor had both tried to talk Elly out of her scheme for robber-catching, but once Elly had an idea in her head there was no shifting it. Surprisingly, Sidney the security guard had been very nice about it.

"Sorry about suspecting you before," he said huskily. "To tell the truth, I'm getting a bit desperate. I can't seem to catch these thieves whatever I do. I need all the help I can get." So Olly and Elly – and Littlest – were helping.

The trouble was they hadn't seen anything suspicious. The Superette was quite small really and it was easy to keep an eye on all of it at once. As far as they could tell, all Mr Patel's customers seemed to be absolutely honest. They came in, pottered round filling their baskets and trolleys, paid up and cleared off. As well as Olly and Elly, there was Sidney the security guard tramping up and down the aisles, and he hadn't seen any stealing either.

Olly was still keen on his idea. "I'm going to take a closer look at that lady," he said. "Maybe I can catch her in the act."

He crept off down the aisle, heading for the fruit section. Littlest decided to go as well. Before Elly could stop him, Littlest jumped out of the bag and set off after Olly.

As Olly crept towards the large lady, Littlest trotted up the aisle, nipped past the astonished Olly, and headed straight for the fruit section.

The large lady was fingering some tomatoes, and Littlest moved round in front of her, hoping she might give him one. Littlest loved tomatoes. When she didn't notice him, Littlest gave a friendly "Eek!" just to let her know he was there.

The lady looked down and saw Littlest looking hopefully up at her. "Eek! Eek! Eek!" said Littlest hungrily, snapping his tiny pointed teeth.

The lady screamed and jumped back – and bumped straight into Olly who was creeping up behind

her. They both reeled backwards, crashing into a big pile of baked bean tins on the other side of the aisle. The pile of tins crashed to the ground, and so did Olly – with the large lady on top of him.

Littlest gave out a panic-stricken "Eek!"

Elly came rushing up with her school bag. "Quick, Littlest," hissed Elly.

Littlest streaked towards the schoolbag and took a flying leap inside, cowering down in the bottom.

The scream and the sound of crashing tins brought Sidney and Mr Patel running to see what was going on. They helped the large lady to her feet. Luckily she was quite unhurt – thanks mostly to Olly who had broken her fall.

"There was a monster, a horrible monster!" screamed the lady. "It was huge!"

"Just a stray dog or cat," said Mr Patel. "See, it has gone now." He looked reproachfully at Elly who stood nearby clutching her schoolbag, looking keenly all around her.

Mr Patel soothed the large lady, gave her a free melon and ushered her from the shop. He came back

and started stacking up the fallen cans. Olly and Elly helped him.

The Professor appeared just as they were finishing.

"I just popped back to see how things were going. Any luck?"

"Total disaster," said Olly gloomily. He told the Professor what had happened. "And we can forget about that lady," he said. "She *is* just as big as she looks. I can guarantee every ounce!"

"I don't think it's any of the customers," said Elly.

"But it must be," said Mr Patel.

Elly shook her head. "This place is so small it's quite easy to check up on. Both of us were watching, and we didn't see a thing. When the cans fell and you and Sidney were both busy it was the perfect chance to steal. No one took anything."

"What do you think is happening then?" asked Mr Patel.

"Well, if the things aren't being stolen by day, then they're disappearing by night," said Elly. "You're being burgled!"

"But that's impossible," said Mr Patel. "There is never any sign of a break in. Burglars would clean out the whole shop."

"Is there anyone here overnight?" asked Olly.

Mr Patel shook his head. "When we close down Sidney checks all the doors and windows. Then I lock the main door and go home. I keep the only set of keys."

"You're being burgled all the same," said Elly. "And if that's the case, it ought to be easy enough to catch them."

"And just how do we do that?" asked Olly.

"Simple," said Elly. "All we have to do is stay in the Superette all night and keep watch!"

Chapter Three

"Eek!" said Littlest.

"Ssh!" said Elly, popping another tomato into the schoolbag at her feet. There was a chomping sound and then silence.

They were sitting in a dark corner of the closed and empty Superette. No one knew they were there, except Mr Patel.

He had lent the Professor his keys so they could all sneak back in after closing-time . . .

The Superette looked strange and spooky in the darkness.

"Still, I've never heard of a haunted supermarket," thought Elly. Olly yawned. "Ssh!" said Elly again.

"You and your mad schemes," muttered Olly.

This particular mad scheme had taken quite a bit of arranging. Elly had persuaded the Professor to ask their parents to let them stay with him overnight. The Professor had

only agreed to help with Elly's plan on condition that he came with them. He was hiding in Mr Patel's little office at the back of the store. If they heard anything suspicious they were to come and tell him at once so he could dial 999.

Elly looked at her watch. The Superette closed at ten, and now it was nearly midnight. Elly was beginning to feel a bit tired. Could she be wrong about the burglars after all?

Littlest decided he'd had enough of sitting in the schoolbag. He was feeling hungry as well. He decided to take a look around.

Elly heard scuffling sounds at her feet and felt inside the schoolbag. She was too late. The bag was empty.

"Oh no!" she whispered.

"What is it?" asked Olly.

"Littlest has gone off somewhere!"

"I'll go and find him," said Olly.

"No, wait," said Elly. "Something's happening."

In the far corner of the Superette a square of light appeared and disappeared. Someone had opened and closed the back door!

Peering through the gloom, they saw a black shape in a balaclava mask moving into the Superette.

They watched in astonishment as the figure took a trolley from the line in the corner and began moving swiftly around the little supermarket, taking just one or two things from each display.

"It's a ghostly shopper," thought Elly. "Maybe the Superette really is haunted!"

Littlest, meanwhile, was prowling round looking for the fruit section. To get a better view he sprang up on to the side of one of the display cases. His claws slipped on the smooth metal and he tumbled inside the case, landing on something round and hard and extremely cold. (Littlest didn't know it, but he'd fallen into a pile of frozen chickens.)

Suddenly, a dark shape loomed over him . . .

Littlest did what many wild creatures do in times of danger. He froze, keeping as still as the strange objects around him . . . Gloved hands picked him up and tossed him into a trolley. Things started landing on top of him, and soon he was almost covered.

Olly and Elly watched as the phantom shopper went on with his midnight shopping. By now he was between them and the office, so they couldn't warn the Professor. And where was Littlest?

The back door opened again and the dark shape wheeled the trolley out into the alley.

Elly grabbed Olly's arm. "Go and tell the Professor to dial 999. I'll follow and see where the burglar goes."

"What about Littlest?"

"He won't go far – we'll have to find him later . . . Go on!"

As Olly headed for the office, Elly snatched up her schoolbag and made for the back door. She opened it quietly and slipped out into the alley, hiding behind some big dustbins. A little van was parked halfway up the alley.

A masked figure was hurling things from the trolley into the van. "Get a move on!" hissed a voice from the driver's seat.

When the trolley was empty, the figure slammed the van doors and wheeled the trolley back into the Superette. It reappeared, closed the back door quietly, and locked it with a key. Then it ran round to the front passenger seat of the van and jumped inside. The van moved away.

The back door opened again and Olly rushed out.

Close behind him was the

Professor, Mr Patel's keys in his hand.

"The police are on their way," he gasped. "What's happening?"

Elly pointed to the little van which was just turning from the alley into the empty high street.

They ran to the end of the alley and watched helplessly as the van drove away.

Littlest struggled free from the pile of stolen shopping and looked around indignantly. He'd been chucked into a shopping trolley, heaved into the van, and now he was being taken off somewhere, away from his friends. Angrily Littlest clambered towards the front of the van . . .

The driver of the van grinned at his partner in crime.

"Another nice one! How many more trips do you reckon we can do?"

Before the other man could answer, a fierce little head appeared from somewhere behind them. The head was on the end of a long thin neck, and it had two rows of sharp-looking teeth.

"Eek!" said Littlest fiercely. "Eek! Eek! Eek!"

"Aaargh!" yelled the driver. "Get it off me!"

Letting go of the wheel he began waving his arms at Littlest. There was a sudden impact and the sound of broken glass . . .

Out in the high street Olly and Elly and the Professor watched in amazement as the van began swerving wildly from side to side. At last it crashed straight into a lamp-post, shattering its windscreen. Olly and Elly started running down the high street towards it.

Inside the van they found the burglars slumped over the

dashboard. The driver was a small, sharp-faced man. Elly had an idea she'd seen him in the Superette. But the tubby figure by his side looked very familiar. Olly pulled off the balaclava mask to reveal the dazed moon-face of Sidney the security guard.

"Eek!" said an indignant voice from inside the van.

Elly opened the door and Littlest jumped out into her arms. There was

the howl of a siren and a police car swung round the corner.

There was just time to pop Littlest back into the bag.

"I suspected Sidney all along," said Elly.

It was much, much later and they were having cheese-and-tomato sandwiches and cocoa in the Professor's house.

Littlest was happily tucking into a plate of tomatoes.

"Oh yes, Sherlock?" said Olly. "How come?"

"Well, I thought he was suspiciously nice when we offered to help," said Elly. "After all, we were more or less taking over his job. And

once it was clear no one was stealing in the daytime, it started to look like an inside job, as we detectives call it!"

"I imagine it started as daytime stealing," said the Professor, "organised by Sidney and that little friend of his. Then Sidney had the bright idea of getting himself taken on as a security guard. He got hold of the keys long enough to make a copy. After that he could do his shoplifting in comfort at night!"

"Good job you got Littlest tucked away before the cops came," said Olly. "A police dog's all very well, but who ever heard of a police dinosaur?"

"Still, he caught the robbers,

didn't he?" said the Professor.

"He certainly did," said Elly. She raised her mug of cocoa. "Here's to Littlest, the world's only dinosaur detective!"

"Eek!" said Littlest happily, and scoffed down another tomato.

[illegible] Young Puffin

Fanny Witch and the Thunder Lizard

Jeremy Strong

[illegible]

Also in Young Puffin

Fanny Witch and the Thunder Lizard

Jeremy Strong

"Oh dear, oh dear. Don't you see? That monster has eaten my Book of Spells. Eaten it!"

Everybody loves Fanny Witch, the schoolteacher, until she magics up a fully grown, live brontosaurus for the children, and the thunder lizard steals her Spell Book so she can't *un*magic the brontosaurus away.

When the boosnatch comes to the village and steals all the children, Fanny Witch has to come to the rescue!

Also in Young Puffin

Adventures of ZOT the DOG

Ivan Jones

Life is fun with Zot!

Zot is a lovable little dog, and he and his friend Clive have all sorts of funny adventures. There's the cheeky mouse who plays tricks on them, a cunning snake who steals all the food, and an unhappy frog who does NOT like being swallowed up by Zot the dog!

Also in Young Puffin

No Prize or Presents for Sam

Thelma Lambert

Sam has always wanted a pet of his own.

Sam sets out to get himself a pet to enter in the Most Unusual Pets Competition at the village fête. But the animal he chooses leads to some very unexpected publicity.

Sam decides it is up to him to give his Aunty and Uncle a happy Christmas when his Aunty loses her job. But how can he earn some money?